In Her Head

A Novelette

D1606557

J.L.E

Dedication

I'd like to take the time to dedicate this book to my mother,
my father, and my significant other. Without them always
pushing me in whatever I chose to do, I wouldn't have had
the courage to actually put my words on paper. Thank you
for everything you've done to help inspire my dreams.

The names of people and events

in this story are fiction.

PART 1

Chapter 1.

The dream came again. She found herself in the dark, wooded, forest.

"Help me, Jade!"

The screaming voice of her twin brother, Jackson, awoke Jade Winters with a start. Heavy breathing, and sweat dripping off her forehead, Jade slowly walked into the kitchen for some fresh cold water. Ever since her brother went missing, she'd been experiencing the same dream, night after night, but there was never an ending. It always began with her chasing after Jackson in a deeply wooded forest, and always ended with him screaming her name. When the dreams come, she's always hoping she will see more. She keeps waiting to see how the dream will end, but it always ends the same way, by waking up when her brother screams.

Her twin brother Jackson up and disappeared one day, almost 6 months ago. He was traveling to New York from their hometown of Green Bay, Wisconsin. He had always wanted to go to New York and be able to finally say he saw the Big Apple. Growing up in Green Bay, Jackson always wanted to spread his wings and venture out and see the world. They weren't sheltered growing up, their family just didn't feel the need to travel much. Jade remembers him begging her to join him on the trip.

"Jade, just think of all the new and exciting things we can see! Big skyscrapers, famous people, concerts!" Jackson excitedly exclaimed to Jade, trying to persuade her. "It'll be exciting and a new adventure that we can enjoy and come back and tell everyone about!"

"Jax, this is more your dream than mine. I'm quite happy staying here and reading in my favorite book shop every day. Plus, you'd be better off experiencing life without your tag along twin sister. "Jade emphasized, hoping Jax would get the picture. "I'll let you enjoy the experience this time." Her brother really was relentless sometimes. He didn't always like to take no for an answer, but he knew when Jade's mind was set, there was no changing it.

Jackson tried almost every day for 2 weeks to get Jade to join him on the bus to New York. She knew it would be hard to leave Green Bay, but it'll be even harder to stay, with Jax leaving her. They've always been side by side growing up. She also wanted her brother to be able to experience life without his nagging sister always harping on him. She knew he needed to do this on his own. Just like she needed to be on her own. They were adults after all, and they couldn't hold each other's hands forever.

As Jade continued drinking her water she glanced outside into the darkness and then at the clock.

"130am, ugh, I need some sleep," she thought to herself as she walked back to her bedroom. 7am will be here before she knows it, and if she doesn't want to be cranky to her coworkers, she needed that rest. She crawled back in bed, pulling the blankets up over her face, and hoping that deep sleep would come fast. She hated when her mind was always full of thoughts of where her brother could be. If he were home, everything would be just fine. She kept repeating "Jax, where are you?" over and over as she finally drifted off to sleep.

Chapter 2.

7am came way too early, Jade was thinking, as she slammed her hand on her alarm clock. Wondering if her job was worth this early morning routine, Jade walked to her closet to grab her outfit for the day. Luckily, working at a hotel reservation call center, she could wear whatever she wanted as long as it was appropriate. She jumped in the shower and then threw on her khakis, short sleeve shirt, and sandals. Throwing her sandy blonde hair in a messy bun, she checked herself in the mirror. While adding some makeup to cover up the bags under her eyes, she double checked herself in the mirror again, and then grabbed her purse and headed for the door.

She stepped out her door and noticed the dreary day in front of her. She made the short walk to her car to jump in and beat traffic to get to work on time. Even at this early hour, traffic was a nightmare. That's what happens in big cities like Green Bay. Rush hour is the absolute worst!

Working with a computer every day, Jade always had access to the internet. In her free time, she was constantly looking up places between Green Bay and New York that might have caught Jackson's attention, to where he would have stayed, instead of finishing his trip. In the last 6 months, she felt the police were giving up their search for him. Every police officer between Green Bay and New York was familiar with Jades name and her missing brother. Jade just felt that they weren't doing enough to help find Jax. Jade binge watched every Detective show she could find, taking notes, and Googling on the internet ways to help look for her brother.

Her main contact she was always transferred too was Detective Michael Lathers. He wasn't a very friendly gentleman, and in person he was even more intimidating. His six" foot stature always loomed over Jades 5'6 frame. She was always intimidated when she saw him. Most of the time he was grouchy and not very sociable. Any time Jade found something, that she felt was important, she called him. She assumed he was getting irritated by her.

Every other day she was calling the police departments asking if there were leads and she always got the same answer, "As soon as we hear or find something, you and your family will be the first to know." This broke Jades heart as well has her parents. Even her mother and father knew this wasn't typical Jackson, he would never just run off without telling anybody or at-least check in. Especially with Jade, their twin relationship made them closer than normal, almost too where they could know what the other one was thinking. If one twin even looked at each other, they would both start laughing. They just had that type of bond.

Jackson was technically born first be a mere 1 minute. But he never failed to bring up that he was the oldest out of the two. It made Jade roll her eyes every time while Jax laughed. Now even as adults at the age of twenty-seven, she still needed to know he was ok. Except Jade was getting that feeling in the pit of her stomach, that he was no ok.

She thought back to their childhood. It was the average, normal childhood. Raised by both parents, who weren't too strict on them, giving them room to learn from their own mistakes. She and Jax were always together and sticking up for each other. When Jade was little, she got made fun of for having glasses, Jax would beat up the bullies. When Jax got his heart broken for the first time, Jade punched the girl. They were always there for each other. Now she wishes that she could rewind time and go back to when they were little again.

Jade let out a heavy sigh as she stepped out of her car to walk into work, and all she could think about was the dreams she'd been having. Part of her was wondering if it was Gods way of helping her figure out where Jax was. The past 2 weeks, she'd been thinking, maybe it was time that she took the same bus route that Jax took. As she got closer to her work cubicle, she saw that there was a blinking light on her phone, meaning she had a voicemail. She put the phone to her ear and dialed her voicemail.

All she heard on the other line was static followed by "Jade, I need you!"

The phone fell out of Jades ear at the sound of the scream on the line. It sounded just like Jacksons scream!

Jade was speechless at first, didn't know what to say. She picked the phone up off the floor and listened to the voicemail again. She listened to it over and over. Her brother was obviously in serious danger. Even he knew to only call Jades work phone in emergencies. She saved the voicemail and called her parents and then the Green Bay Police

Department. Maybe now, the search for her brother would

be taken seriously!

Chapter 3.

The Green Bay Police Department sent down Detective Lathers, of course, to listen to and record the voicemail left on Jades phone. He said they were going to see if there was any way to track where the call came from. Jade noticed the look on his face as soon as he walked in, looking like he wasn't too thrilled to be there.

"Jade, we will do our best to see if we can trace that call. But with this being a call center, it will be tough to triangulate the area where that call came from." Lathers stated, peering at Jade. "You guys receive calls from every state, some from out the country. That's what makes this a little bit more difficult."

"Isn't there anyway at all to pinpoint the vicinity down?" Jade asked with hopeful eyes. Almost begging.

"Unfortunately, I can't promise that. But we will do our best to try. We will notify your parents and you if we are able to gain any leads." He shook her hand, while handing her a business card with his other hand. "If anything, else happens, call me." He said to Jade while turning to leave the building.

Jade went about her day, but every call that came in, she was hoping it was her brother on the other end of the phone. She had the worst feeling in the pit of her stomach that Jax needed her. Making it through her 8-and-a-half-hour shift was twice as hard today. No matter how hard she tried to focus on her work, it got harder and harder for her mind to not wander back to her dreams and this morning's voicemail. She listened to it again. She was getting increasingly angry every time she listened to it, but for some reason she just couldn't stop.

Detective Lathers reached out to Jade around noon, to let her know that they weren't able to track the call from her brother. Jade was getting more frustrated by the minute. She kept telling herself that she couldn't blame Detective Lathers, because he was just doing his job.

When the clock struck 330pm, Jade was clocking out of her shift and making her way out the door. She was debating on stopping at her book shop today, but didn't know if she was in the mood, and she felt that she couldn't really focus on a book right now. As she was walking to her car in the parking lot, she kept getting that uneasy feeling that she was being watched. She stopped and turned around.

"Is anyone there?" Silence.

Jade kept walking. She walked to her car, unlocked the door, and climbed in. She put on her seat belt and started the car. As she went to adjust her rear-view mirror, she looked in it, and saw someone in the mirror. Wearing all black, hood over their head, Jade jumped. They were staring straight at her. She looked down to find her phone to call the police, and when she looked back in the rear-view mirror, they were gone. Whoever it was, they were definitely fast. Jade put her phone down, put her car in reverse, backed out, and sped away.

On the drive home, once again, Jade couldn't shake the feeing she was being followed. Once she reached her home, she pulled into the garage, got out of her car, and ran inside. First thing she did was check all the doors and windows, making sure everything was locked. Once she felt safe, she sat on the couch, trying to catch her breath. When she was checking the windows, she didn't notice the black van that had parked down the street from her house.

Someone was watching. Someone was waiting.

Chapter 4.

Once again it was 130am and Jade was up pacing her living room floor. Her recurring dream happened again, and with today's events, her mind was going every direction. Jade was starting to wonder if the person she saw in her rear-view mirror today, had something to do with her brother's disappearance.

BANG! BANG!

Jade jumped as a loud banging knock came from her front door. "Who would be pounding on my door at 130am?" Jade asked herself as she started walking to her front door. She looked through the peep hole but didn't see anything. She opened up the door and noticed an envelope hanging by the doorknob. She opened it and gasped at what she read. There on the piece of paper were the words:

<u>YOU'RE NEXT.</u>

Jade ran back inside the house and locked her door. She sat the envelope and paper down on the coffee table in the living room. She started looking for Detective Lathers business card that he gave to her this afternoon. She called the number listed. She could hear the Detective fumbling with the phone trying to answer.

"This is Detective Lathers." He answered sounding half asleep.

"Detective Lathers, this is Jade, and something really strange just happened at my house." She went into detail of the day's events, when she left work, and the pounding on her door with the envelope she found. He instructed her to put on gloves and place it in a Ziploc bag. Then he instructed Jade to take it to the police department for fingerprints and he would meet her there and take her statement.

Jade quickly through on some comfortable clothes, did what the Detective instructed and raced down to the police station. While driving, Jade tried to call her parents, but there was no answer. Assuming they were sleeping, she left them a voicemail explaining what happened. Just as she hung up the phone, she pulled into the police station parking lot.

As she was walking inside, she didn't notice the black van that was driving past her. She met Detective Lathers at the front desk when she walked in. She handed him the Ziploc bag and let out of big breath, that she hadn't realized she was holding. He had her walk with him into an interview room so she could give her statement.

"Jade, I can see that you're really shaken up," he says as he sees Jade trembling and looking anxious. "It's understandable, but I need you to calm down and take some deep breaths and try to explain today's events. Also tell me about the events that happened within the last hour." Lathers told Jade as she was sitting down at the table, letting out a breath of relief, and started to recap everything that happened today.

Lathers wrote down Jades statement and got her something to drink.

"We are going to see if we can run the envelope or paper for fingerprints. I sent it down to the lab, and we should know within a few days, hopefully, if anyone handled it besides you." The Detective informed her.

Jade nodded her head up and down, acknowledging what they were doing. She shook his hand and walked out the door to head home. As she got into her car, she was spent. All of today's events, and the last 2 weeks of dreams, waking her up every night. She felt beat. She pulled into her garage and walked inside. Double checking doors and windows, she walked to her bedroom, looked at the clock saying 415am, rolled her eyes and crawled in bed.

"I'm calling into work tomorrow and I'm going to go look for my brother myself." She started thinking of what she needed to start with. First thing tomorrow morning, she was going to get a bus ticket to New York. Taking Jacksons exact, same route. In the past 6 months since Jackson has been missing, Jade kept thinking about just driving the route. She was afraid if she drove though, she would miss some chances of talking to certain people that her brother could have come in contact with. She didn't want to miss those chances. She was going to follow his steps.

Chapter 5.

Jade was up bright and early the next morning scrolling on her laptop. She was on the verge of confirming her bus ticket. Leaving on the same day of the week, taking the exact route that Jackson had taken. As she was entering in her credit card numbers, her mind skipped back to the day Jax got on the bus.

It was a sunny June day as Jade and her parents' said goodbye to Jackson as he got on the bus.

"Be sure to check in as soon as you get to New York!" Their mother emphasized as she was hugging him, more tightly than he liked. Once she let go, his dad shook his hand and reminded him to be careful. Then it was Jades turn.

"You still have time to come along Jade." He said one last time, pleading with his big, blue eyes.

"No thanks Jax, you're on your own on this adventure." He hugged her quick and ran to give his ticket to the driver. As he got to his seat, he pulled open the window, waving with his cheesy grin. They stood there waving until they could no longer see the bus. They walked back to the car in silence. It would be 1 week later, when they learn that Jackson had never checked into the place he was supposed to be staying in New York.

Jade snapped back to reality as she was printing her ticket off the computer. She had everything planned out and was ready to show she meant business. She was thoughtful and decided to let Detective Lathers and her parents know what she was doing. Jade assumed it was safe to say, that neither party agreed with what she was about to do.

"You need to leave this to the police!" Lathers had scolded, but Jade ignored his warning. With his attitude and demeanor, last thing she wanted to do was listen to him.

"What if something happens to you, then we will have two missing children. I won't allow it!" Her father had shouted while her mother cried.

As much as both parties rejected her decision, it was still her decision to make. It came down to the fact that he was her brother, and something had to be done. She knew in her heart that Jax would do the same thing for her, had their roles had been switched. Even though they were against the idea, her parents accompanied her to the bus station the morning her bus was set to leave.

It was a dreary, December day as her parents were walking with her over to the bus stop. For Wisconsin, it was a normal, December day.

"Please call at every stop!" Her mother insisted, while giving her a great big hug.

"Are you sure you won't change your mind?" This is something the police should be handling!" Her dad said, begging her to stay. She kissed him on the cheek.

"This is something I need to do, then maybe, I'll be able to get some answers for us." Jade reassured them. She hugged them both one more time and continued walking to the bus.

She waved as she walked onto the bus platform. She gave her ticket to the driver and found her seat. She then opened her window and waved to her parents as the bus pulled out of the terminal. She grabbed her bus route out of her carryon pack and looked it over for the millionth time. First stop: Columbia County, Wisconsin. Columbia was roughly a 2-and-a-half-hour drive from Green Bay. It would be the last stop until Chicago., which was another 5-hour drive after Columbia County.

Jades cell phone started to ring for an incoming text, just as she was getting comfortable on the bus. It was Detective Lathers. He informed Jade that there weren't any hits for fingerprints on the envelope and paper found at her house. Jade set her cell phone down while frowning. "Of course not, because that would be too easy." She said out loud to herself, sarcastically.

As Jade grabbed her headphones out of her bag, she looked over at the person sitting on the other side of the aisle wearing a baseball hat and black hoodie. He glanced over and waved hello. She waved back as she put her headphones on and leaned back in her seat. "Please let this trip give me some answers or closure at least." She said to herself as her tired eyes slowly drifted to sleep.

Chapter 6.

Jade was running through the forest following Jackson as fast as she could, losing light faster and faster as darkness came upon her. She started screaming for Jax

"Jax! Jax, where are you?!" Not paying attention, she tripped over something on the ground, trying to catch herself she went down with a thud. As she scrambled to get back on her feet, she glanced over at what she tripped over. It was something long and dark, as she got closer to it, she realized whatever it was, it was wrapped in a dark blue blanket. As she got closer something reached out and touched her from behind. She screamed.

Jade opened her eyes, and she was staring at the gentleman from the next aisle. He had his hand on her shoulder. He was lucky she didn't punch him out of pure reflex.

"You were screaming in your sleep, I just wanted to wake you up, and make sure you were ok." He clarified.

"Bad dream. Sorry." She said, embarrassed, while looking around at the people on the bus, gazing at her. She tried to hide her red face and sunk back into the seat, hoping people wouldn't stare to long.

"My name is Gavin." The gentleman said as he sat next to her. Jade scooted closer to the window, not wanting to be too close to this stranger. He came off grungy and kind of scary looking with his oily dark hair and dressed all in black.

"Jade." She piped back, not really in the mood for conversation with a stranger.

"I'm heading to New York City, where about are you headed off to?" Gavin asked.

"Same, just making some stops along the way." Jade felt odd giving this stranger so much information, so she kept it short and to the point.

Gavin must have thought she wasn't too talkative, so he politely stood up and said "Well I'm going to let you finish your nap. Enjoy the rest of the ride, and it was nice to meet you." As he walked back to his seat.

Jade didn't get a chance to say goodbye, but she did feel a little awful for getting snippy with the gentleman. He apparently just wanted someone to talk to, but Jade just had too many things on her mind, and she didn't feel like going into all the details. She didn't want people to feel sorry for her, because she's out looking for her lost brother. Jade wasn't a fan of pity parties. Plus, she was also getting a creepy vide from Gavin. Wearing all black and tightly holding on to the backpack in his lap, he kept making glances over at Jade, which was really starting to get on her nerves. She was trying so hard not to yell at him for staring at her. The last thing she wanted to do was cause a scene on the bus.

Jade turned her attention to the window for a sign to see where they were. Luck would have it; a sign came up that said Columbia County: twelve miles. She sighed, glad that the first stop was almost here. She really needed to stretch her legs and grab a snack.

She grabbed at her bag on the floor, to take out the list she had made of all the closest places next to the bus stops on the route. She brought the latest picture she had of Jackson to ask around to see if anyone saw him. She prayed at least one person could remember him in Columbia County, and especially to see if he even got back on the bus there, to head to the next stop on the route to New York.

The thing about Jackson he was hard to forget, especially for the ladies. His sandy blonde hair and his bright blue eyes always got the girls attention. Every time Jade would give him a hard time about it, he would blush and look away. Jade had the same hair and same eyes, plus glasses, but she didn't get near as much attention from the guys like her brother got from the ladies. Jade grinned just thinking about it.

Jade yawned as she stretched her arms to stand up as the bus pulled into the bus terminal. They had 2 hours before it took off to the next destination of their trip, which was Chicago. Jade scanned around to see where she'd head to first when she saw this cute, little, corner café next to the bus terminal. She was thinking that would be a great place to start her search. As she started walking that way, she got that queasy feeling she was being followed again, glancing around just to be sure, she shook off the feeling as she walked in the front door of the café.

Chapter 7.

The sweet smell of apple pie caught her attention as soon as she walked into the café. She approached the counter and saw a sweet little old lady behind the counter, name tag said Betty. The café must be a fairly good place to eat, Jade thought as she glanced around. There didn't seem to be many empty seats.

"Good evening dearie, what will you be having?" The sweet lady asked as Jade walked up to the counter.

"That apple pie smells delicious; can I get a slice of that?" Jade answered while eying the pie, ever so hungry.

"You bet hon, coming right up. Grab yourself a seat and it'll be over to you in a jiffy." Betty exclaimed.

Jade found a window booth unoccupied and grabbed a seat and pulled her backpack next to her. She took out Jax's photo to be able to ask the waitress if she happened to see him or remember him, while checking to see how much time she had before the bus departed.

Betty walked over with a smile on her face and the most delicious looking piece of pie Jade had ever seen. Betty was also nice enough to bring a big cup of coffee, which Jade didn't realize she needed until she was taking that first drink.

"Sweetheart, you look plum wore out. You are traveling?" Betty asked making conversation, Jade assumed.

"Yes, ma'am I am. I'm from Green Bay, Wisconsin heading to New York, on the bus. I'm actually looking for my brother Jackson, he would've been by here at this time about

6 months ago." Jade informed Betty, as she was reaching for Jax's picture.

"Have you by chance see him?" Jade asked while handing Betty the picture.

"Unfortunately, my memory isn't the best, but can I see that picture to ask the other girls working?" Betty asked Jade.

"Absolutely!" Jade said as she handed Betty the picture. "Anything would help, anything at all!"

"I'll be back with it shortly!" Betty said as she walked back to the counter by the other waitresses. Jade could see them talking but couldn't make out what they were saying. Jade started to take a piece from her pie, when she saw Betty walking back towards her.

"Sadly, the girls don't remember if they saw him. But after looking at this for a while, I do vaguely remember a young gentleman that looks a lot like this picture, and a lot like you." Betty informed her.

"We are twins; I just happen to have glasses." Jade said while shrugging her shoulders. "Did he seem off at all, or nervous, scared, anything of the sort?"

Betty answered, "Not that I noticed. He ordered some pie and chocolate milk, and then I left him and his friend to their conversation. I do remember how sweet and polite he was. Don't get many of them kind around here." Betty added.

Friend? Jade thought.

"Can you tell me what this friend looked like, Betty?"

"I remember he had a bandana and was wearing a black sweatshirt. That's really all I can remember of the young man. I'm sorry I can't be more help." Betty said with a frown.

"Oh no you've been wonderful Betty! Thanks so much for all you help!" Jade said cheerfully as she shook Betty's hand. "Can I give you my cell phone number in case you remember anything else?"

"Certainly dear." Betty said as Jade handed her the number, written on a piece of napkin.

"That pies on the house dear. I'll be praying you find some information about your brother, just be careful. People tend to go missing around here." Betty said with a small smile while walking away from the table.

Jade took notes of everything Betty told her as she gulped down the apple pie followed by the coffee. She looked out the window at the bar across the street and then at her watch to check how much time she had left to ask questions. She had a little over an hour to kill yet and the bar would be her next stop.

She glanced at the bulletin board by the door on the way out. The waitress was right, there were a lot of missing posters. They all looked close to Jade and Jackson's age. Something seemed off about this place. "Why are there so many missing people's posters?" Jade asked herself. She looks at the posters one more time before walking out the door of the café.

Chapter 8.

Jade started thinking as she made her way across the street to the bar that her last dream on the bus got farther than the rest. It made her start to wonder if there was a connection, as she's looking for her brother. Maybe taking this trip was just the thing she needed. Maybe the closer she got to him, the further the dreams got. She hoped this was a good sign, because she certainly needed some good signs right now.

Jade tensed up as she started to walk into the bar. She relaxed when she realized there was only one person in there, the bartender. He looked at her funny as she walked up to the bar.

"Can I get you something?" He asked with a tone.

"Just some answers if possible." As she brought out Jax's photo. "Have you seen this man in the last 6 months?

"He kind of resembles a man that came in once, a while back, but I didn't catch his name." He told Jade.

Jade gasped. "Resembles? Like how??"

"The hair is kind of the same but a little darker. Eyes are pretty close, but he looked higher than a kite so I can't be too sure, and he had a hoodie over his head." The man shrugged.

That's impossible. Jades brother didn't do drugs, he never touched them. Even when they were younger and other people started doing them. That was one thing they swore they would never touch.

"He came in with that thug friend of his, who's always causing trouble." The bartender said back, his voice a little sterner now.

"How can you remember that long ago?" Jade asked out of curiosity.

"Because his friend is an asshole, always causing trouble when he's in here. Not sure how people can put up with him!" He snapped back at Jade.

"Do you by chance know where I could possibly find this thug friend?"

"If you come back around 11pm, you might catch him in here. Can't miss him, he's always doing something up to no good. He's in here almost every night causing some kind of trouble."

"I'll definitely be back." Jade informed the bartender. Guess that means she wasn't going to be getting on the bus for the next stop. As she stepped out of the bar, she looked around for a place to crash. Seeing a vacancy sign on the Motel 6 sign, she decided she would go book a room, at least for tonight. She went to grab her belongings off the bus, informed the driver she was staying and went to her seat to retrieve her headphones and carryon bag.

As she got closer, she realized there was an envelope on her seat with her name on it. It looked oddly familiar. As she opened the envelope and read what it said, she tried not to scream.

<u>Quit looking.</u>

That's all the notes said. Jade looked around to see if anyone had noticed. She asked some passengers if they had seen who dropped it off, but no one had because they just got back on the bus. Whoever left it, did it when nobody else was around.

She asked the bus driver one more time if he had seen her brother and again, he should his head no. She went to step off the bus and bumped into Gavin, spilling his drink all over himself.

"I'm so sorry Gavin!" Jade apologized while trying to find something to help dry him off.

"It's ok, it'll dry. What's the hurry is there a fire somewhere?" Gavin asked jokingly.

"No, I was just being clumsy." Not wanting to give more details, Jade said sorry again and was starting to walk away.

"Wait. Where are you going, the bus is almost ready to leave?" Gavin called out after her.

"That's ok, I'm staying. I have some things to do." She yelled back at him over the loud noise of the bus starting.

When she looked back, she realized he was still staring at her, as she rounded the corner, by the café, to head to the motel.

Chapter 9.

While checking into a room at the Motel 6, Jade asked
the motel worker if they had, by chance, seen her brother,
and of course it was a no. After she got the key to her room,
she went to go find it. In the back of her mind, she was
hoping that she didn't mess up, by staying here in Columbia
County, and not getting back on the bus. Hoping this wasn't
a dead end. There are quite a few gentlemen that could
resemble Jax, especially with that blonde hair and blue eyes.
Jade smacked herself in the head as she scanned her card to

get into her room. Nothing fancy but good enough for one night, hopefully.

She glanced at her watch, 3 hours until 11pm, she might as well freshen up, and it might help her calm her nerves. She turned on the television for noise, dug through her bag for some clothes, and decided to run a nice, hot, bubble bath. Nothing beats soaking in a bubble bath, Jade thought to herself as she started to undress.

Jade slowly got into the bathtub and sat down in the bubbles, tilted her head back and put a washcloth over her eyes. Nothing wrong with a snooze in the bathtub, Jade told herself. She was so nervous wondering how this evening was going to go, and the thought of possibly finding Jax. She just wanted to relax for a few minutes and try to remain positive about the situation.

"Your so close Jade, please help me" Jax yelled.

Jade abruptly woke up breathing heavy. She could have sworn she heard Jax yell in this very room. She realized she was still in the bathtub and must have dozed off for a little while because the water was starting to get cold. She pulled the drain plug, grabbed a towel, and lifted herself out of the tub. Glancing at the clock by the bed, she realized it was 9pm. She dozed off for an hour in the tub!

Jade started pulling her clothes on piece by piece. She didn't want to draw any attention to herself in a bar she knew nothing about, or anyone in it. She threw on some comfortable jeans and a long sleeve shirt and did a quick look in the mirror, to make sure she looked halfway decent. She remembered to call her parents as she was flicking through channels on the hotel television. It was a quick conversation as she didn't want them to worry, so she didn't fill them in on what she was about to do. She let them think she was still on the bus. They exchanged their 'I love Yous" with each other and hung up the phone.

Jade spent the next hour and a half, pacing her room, wishing time would go faster. Her heart was racing, her nerves all worked up. In the back of her mind, she could feel this town had a connection to Jax. Almost every place she's been here, so far, has brought up this so-called friend of his. Who is this friend? And what does he know about Jackson's disappearance? Jade didn't know but she was going to find out, and this so-called friend, better be ready to give some straight answers.

Chapter 10.

Jade watched television until the clock read 1055pm, then threw on her jacket and headed out the door to the bar. Luckily it was only a block, because it was December, and it was cold. As she walked across the street to the bar, she got that strange feeling she was being followed again. She turned around.

"Hello? Is anybody there?" All Jade got back was silence. She finished her walk to the bar.

Jade walked in and found an empty table in the back. It was definitely crowded now, Jade thought as she saw the bartender from earlier glance her way. When he saw her, he started to walk her way.

As he approached her table he said "The guy I was telling you about is back by the pool table. He's wearing a dark blue hoodie and a bandana on his head. Do you see him?"

Jade quickly darted her eyes that direction without being too obvious. She saw the man alright. He didn't look familiar, and the way he looked actually intimidated Jade. But she wasn't going to let him know that. Jade could be tough when she needed to be, and this was the time that she needed to be.

She told the bartender thanks and ordered a sex on the beach to drink. If she was going to be in the bar, then she needed to look the part. Jade figured out her strategy and how she was going to play this off to be able to talk to the gentleman. At least trying not to give anything away. When the waitress brought her drink, Jade chugged it down, put her glasses in her purse, and started her walk to the pool table.

As she got closer to the pool table, she pretended to be a little wobbly, so she could pass off as being somewhat drunk. Then she "accidentally" bumped into this "friend" of Jacksons as he was taking his turn at pool.

"What the hell?" He cussed while turning around and seeing Jade, then his frown turned to a smile.

"I'm sooooooo sorry, I seem to be a little clumsy this evening" Jade said, playing it off while slurring her words.

"That's ok darling shows your having a good time. What's a pretty little things like you doing in here all by your lonesome?"

"My friends wanted to leave, and I wasn't ready. Told them I'd get a cab."

"Well better stick with me so nothing happens to you," he grinned. "What's your name sweetheart?"

"Roxie, what's yours?" Jade lied, not wanting to give her name away in case this guy had talked to Jax.

"Cooper, and it's wonderful to meet you." He said as he put his arm around her shoulders.

Jade started feeling ill at the gesture. She excused herself to go to the restroom. "Hurry back" Cooper called after her. She rushed into the stall and sat down to get her head straight. You're doing this for Jackson, she kept telling herself. She freshened up her face with water and headed back to Cooper. When she got back to the pool table, Cooper handed her a drink and asked her to dance. She politely accepted, took a sip of her drink and followed Cooper to the dance floor. She was unaware that Cooper had slipped something in her drink while she was in the restroom.

After a couple dances, Jades head started to feel dizzy, to the point that she wasn't able to even see straight. She hardly could see Cooper leading her out of the bar and into his pickup. Once inside the truck, half asleep, Jade tried to get out, but the doors were locked. She started to yell when Cooper put his hands over her mouth, "Shut up if you want to survive the night", she bit down hard, digging her teeth into his hand to get him to let go.

"You bitch!" He screamed at Jade, before punching her in the face, and then everything went black.

Chapter 11.

"What the fuck am I supposed to do with her?" Cooper said loudly to someone on the phone, as Jade started to come to, hearing all the commotion. She pretended to still be knocked out so she could hear more of the conversation. She heard screaming on the other end of the phone, but couldn't make out any of the words, but whoever it was sounded angry.

"I don't know what she's doing here, but I found a picture in her purse of one of the last kids we got off the bus." He said into his cell phone more quietly this time.

Jax! Jade thinking to herself, "Please let him be ok."

"If I let her go, it ruins the whole operation. What if she squeals?" Cooper was on the verge of starting to panic.

"You're the boss. We will be there shortly." Cooper said as he hung up the phone.

"Stupid bitch!" He said out loud to himself.

They'd been driving in Cooper's truck for what seemed like forever, after many turns, they finally came to a stop. Jade didn't want to open her eyes, because she was afraid of what was going to happen.

"I know you're awake, I can see your eyes flinching." Cooper said to her while shaking her shoulder.

Jade opened her eyes as good as she could, but the right one was swollen shut. She rubbed the right side of her face where Cooper had punched her. "Ouch" she said wincing.

"Be careful, or the left side will match it. Don't do anything stupid." He expressed to her, as he got out of the pickup. He got out and made his way over to Jades door, opened it, and motioned for her to get out. She was scared and didn't want too, but he grabbed her by the arm and pulled her out. When he reached, that was when she noticed the sight of the pistol in his belt.

As she balanced on her feet to regain her posture, she looked around at what she could make out with one eye. Looked like we were in the middle of a forest, and we were standing right in front of a cabin. If this weren't such a terrible predicament, she thought it'd be almost pretty. Snapping back to reality, Cooper pushed Jade to start walking towards the cabin.

"What are you going to do with me?" Jade asked Cooper.

"Well, if you're lucky, maybe not kill you. But what happens is technically up to how well you are at cooperating." Cooper told her, but not reassuringly. "That's really up to the boss, I don't get to make those decisions." Jade was getting the feeling that Cooper was upset he didn't have more say, in whatever operation he was involved with.

"Stop walking." Cooper instructed Jade as he put a blindfold over her eyes.

"What's this for?" Jade asked with hesitation.

"To avoid you from seeing anything you're not supposed to, in case we decide to let you live, but even that idea is still iffy." Cooper replied back.

He helped her walk through the door of the cabin, and sat Jade on a chair, and proceeded to tie her arms behind her back. Jade was trying to dig deeper into her senses, for noises, and smells, in case she made it out alive to tell the police.

"What took you so fucking long Cooper?" Jade heard a deeper voice yell at Cooper, as a hand pounded on a table. Why did that voice sound familiar?

"Well, my truck runs like shit, I've been drinking, and I kidnapped someone, so sorry if I didn't want to get pulled over by the po-pos!" Cooper said standing his ground.

"Don't back talk me you piece of shit. Now get downstairs and do your job!" The voice got louder. Jade jumped.

"Yes sir, boss." She heard Cooper say sarcastically.

Jade heard steps waking away and started to relax a little, thinking she might actually be alone. Just then she felt a hand on her shoulder, and she jumped. As someone started pulling her blindfold down, even with one eye, Jade could make out who it was.

"Why, hello Jade, how nice of you to visit." Detective Lathers said with a smirk, as a lump formed in the back of Jades throat.

Chapter 12.

Jade was speechless.

"Cat got your tongue Jade. I said to let the police handle it, but you just couldn't do that could you? Had to go and try to save the day." Lathers got louder as he leaned his face closer to Jades.

"I don't even know what you're doing, I'm just looking for my brother." Jade pleaded.

"Well, your brother now works for me, and I will admit, he put up quite a fight, but enough beatings and drugs wore him down, but by then he had no idea what he was doing. He's so far gone he won't even know you!" Lathers said back.

"You've known where he was this whole time? Couldn't you have just told me he was alive?" Jade asked.

"Why would I do that? He's been quite handy to have around. Hard worker. And well it's shocking my little scare tactics didn't persuade you to stay put. Jax got a cell phone a couple times because some workers were too fucking stupid and left it lying around, but like I said, with the beatings and drugs I don't expect him to make that mistake again." He yelled so loud so everyone could hear him, but Jade didn't see anyone else.

"Fucking Cooper!" Lathers yelled shaking his head, acknowledging whose cell phone it must have been that Jax got ahold of.

"If you just let me, go, I promise I won't tell anyone anything. I don't even know what you're doing!" Jade pleaded again.

Just then, Jade heard some yelling from what sounded like underneath her feet. "God damnit", Lathers cussed. "Fucking stay put". He pointed his finger at Jade then he walked into another room. Jade heard him screaming at whoever was yelling. "Shut your fucking mouth. And you, do your job or you'll be the next one dead." Lathers issued a threat to someone, and then it got quiet.

Next one dead? Jade was starting to worry even more. How was she going to get out of here?

While Jade had a chance, she moved her arms up and down behind the chair to see if there was anything sticking out of it, to possibly help loosen or cut the rope around her wrists. She thought she felt a nail, but by the time she found it Lathers was walking towards her, almost like he appeared out of nowhere, so she quickly quit moving. She didn't want him to notice that she was looking for a way to escape, afraid of what he might do if he got too angry.

"Now what to do with you." He said while sitting down in a chair across from her. "I could let you go but that'd be too easy and too risky. I could kill you but that's too much effort. I think you'll be our next little helper." He said with a grin spreading across his face. "I imagine you're a hard worker just like your brother. We can always use more of those."

Chapter 13.

"Are you the reason for all the missing people's posters in town?" Jade asked, hoping to get some more information, to give back to the police. If she made it out of here alive, that is.

"Saw those did you? Yea, I can't take all the credit. Cooper was actually an exceptionally good lackey for those. He was pretty persuasive when he met people getting off the buses for their break. Younger adults tend to head for the nearest bar on a long bus trip, and Cooper knows how to slip stuff into drinks when people aren't looking. Take you for example." Lathers pointed out.

"Now let me show you what we are doing out here in the middle of nowhere." Lathers told her and he pulled her up out of the chair, holding a gun to her back, he undid the ropes, he pushed her in front of him and told her where to go.

"Walk into this kitchen and under the table you'll see a door, open it and walk down the ladder." Jade did as she was told.

It was dark until she reached the bottom of the ladder, and she turned around and her mouth dropped. She was staring at tables and tables of a white powdery substance, and at least a dozen people, one at each table wearing masks, and almost practically naked. There were armed gentleman walking by all the tables, overlooking, to make sure everyone was doing what they were supposed to be doing. There were bricks of the white substance lined up again the far west wall.

"What is all this?" Jade asked, not quite sure, but assuming.

"Well, you should know, but this is cocaine Jade. I'm the biggest cocaine dealer for the Midwest and the eastern side of the United States." Lathers said while laughing.

"You kept my brother here to help you package cocaine?" Jade yelled as she spit in his face.

"Oh, he does more than that. He also deals it for us, but he really doesn't have a choice." Lathers replied while wiping off his face. "He's not really all there anymore, the drugs will do that to you." He said as he looked to the right of him. Jade followed his gaze and down at the very end of the last table was her brother. She couldn't believe her eyes. He didn't even look the same anymore. He looked so skinny and sickly looking.

"Jackson!" Jade screamed. It was like he didn't even hear her. Lathers laughed.

"Don't you get it Jade? All my workers are nobodies. Nobody's looking for them, thinking the police, myself, are looking for them. It's the perfect cover. Nice little hideout out in the middle of nowhere. No one around for miles. No one to hear any screams or gunshots. I could bury your brother or you for that matter and it would take a hell of a lot longer than a few days for anyone to find you." Lathers said with a smile on his face.

"If you would've just stayed in Green Bay, this could have all been avoided." He reiterated to her.

"How are you able to do both? You can't be a police officer full time, and be a drug producer?" Jade asked, curious to how he's been able to get away with it.

"Jade, I'm a cop. I'm supposed to be working this case, I have all the excuses in the world to be a measly, two and a half hours away from my location. I also have the clearance. I'm able to get away with a lot more than you give me credit for." He said, smiling.

Jade asked "So now what happens? You obviously aren't going to let me go if you showed me all this."

"You're right, so you'll end up just like the rest of them." He stated. No sooner did the words escape his mouth, then there came a loud noise from upstairs.

BOOM!

Lathers jumping at the noise, looked at 2 of his guards and nodded his head for them to check it out. As soon as they stepped upstairs off the ladder, there were gun shots. Jade screamed and took off towards her brother. The others took off running in any direction they could.

"What the hell is going on up there?!" Lathers screamed while running up the ladder and locking it from the inside. He yelled at a guard by the nearest table. "Grab as much as you can and meet me at the docks!" He instructed. Jade watched him disappear through a secret tunnel, in the wall, behind a refrigerator.

"Jax, look at me!" She said while grabbing his head with her hands and pulling his face towards her. She looked into his blue eyes. "Please Jax, it's me Jade, your sister, your twin sister! You have to remember me!" She said, crying while screaming, to drown out the gun shots upstairs. Jackson didn't say anything just looked at Jade with dead eyes, almost like a zombie. She grabbed him and went out the same way she saw Lathers go. They came out through a cave that led back into the forest. Jade recognized this forest from the dreams she'd been having. She wasn't seeing the cabin close by at all, so she wasn't sure exactly where they were in the forest.

Chapter 14.

As both Jade and Jackson started walking in the forest not sure where to go, Jade realized just how dark it was. With no light to guide them, Jade kept ahold of Jackson's hand, so they stayed together in the dark. After walking for about 10 minutes Jade saw a shadow standing in front of them. It was Lathers and he was pointing his gun right at her.

"I'm not going to let you ruin everything I've worked for these last few years." He aimed his gun to shoot. Jade grabbed Jax and took off running into the trees. She heard

the shot ring out, but it missed. Not knowing what direction

Lathers went in, they kept running until Jade tripped over

something in her path. As she stood up and turned around,

she realized it was the same thing that she tripped over in her

last dream. Whatever it was, was wrapped in a blue blanket.

Jade decided now was the time to figure out what it was.

Jade got closer and reached down to unwrap the

blanket. As she did, a stench from inside it was starting to

come out. She kept unraveling, while trying not to vomit.

When it finally came to the very end, Jade screamed a blood

curdling scream. She was staring at the face of her twin

brother, wrapped in the blue blanket on the ground.

"This can't be! Jax!" Jade said out loud as she turned

around. She came face to face with someone else that

happened to look a lot like Jackson. "NOOO!" Jade let out a

scream.

"Jade?! Jade!" Jade heard someone screaming her

name. "Where are you, Jade?" They got closer. "There you

are!" Jade looked up and looked right into Gavin's eyes. He was holding Lathers in handcuffs.

"What are YOU doing here?" Jade asked confused. "I'm FBI Jade, I've been following you this whole time." Gavin reassured her by showing his badge. Jade went to stand up off the ground, looking down again at her brother's body and fainting right into Gavin's arms.

1 month later

The funeral, for Jackson was long overdue and very heavily populated. There were people standing outside the church due to not enough room inside. People, Jade hadn't seen in years, were coming to pay their respects to her brother. Jackson did have that ever lasting effect on people. Jade gave the eulogy and Jackson would have been so proud of her, especially since she didn't like to speak in front of big groups of people. She knew she could handle it for her brother.

It took some time for Jade's parents to cope with losing Jackson. A parent should never have to bury a child, it should be the other way around. Jade's mom and dad tried to put all their attention on Jade being safe and home, before really processing the fact that Jackson was really gone.

It took a while for the body to be released to Jade's family due to it being part of an investigation. Jade was able to collect his belongings from the police department while she was there giving her statement.

Gavin was able to give Jade all the details once everything had been reported to the police department. The first gun shots Jade heard in the cabin, was the FBI firing at the armed guards outside. Once that started it all escalated really fast. Then one of Lathers hired men squealed about his secret tunnel out of the basement into the cave, which made it a lot easier to track him down.

"How did you even know what was going on?" Jade asked Gavin, the day after Jackson's funeral.

"Well, we've been working on the missing people's case down in Columbia County. We had information on Cooper, but we weren't sure who the big boss in charge was. We found that out, that night when you were taken. When the FBI heard you were going to be going to look for Jackson yourself, I was specifically assigned to watch you during your trip. I started before you left."

"How did you follow me though? You were on the bus." Jade pointed out to him.

"No, you walked away before watching the bus depart. Therefore, you didn't see me actually getting into a 4-door black van. I've followed your every move, making sure I could jump in at any time." I'm sorry I was a little late." He apologized looking at her with his dark green eyes. Jade realized how handsome he was when he was all cleaned up in his FBI suit. An enormous difference from his grungy bus look.

"So, was that Lathers that was trying to scare me in Green Bay?" Jade asked, hoping he knew the answer.

"Yes, it was. He told us, that he was trying to scare you off. He was worried that you would find out what he was doing and ruin his money-making scheme. He was right to worry, because of you, he won't be making money anytime soon." Gavin said with a big smile forming on his face.

"It's weird, Lathers thought Jackson was still working for him. How could he not know that he was already dead?" Jade asked, puzzled.

"Lathers didn't pay enough attention. The kid that you brought out, looked a lot like Jackson, especially when they were drugged up. The kid you brought out, his name was Trevor. Thanks to you, he's back with his family. Thanks to you, they are all back with their families. All the people you saw in that drug den, were on the missing posters." Gavin told Jade, giving her a little comfort.

"What about the voicemail I got at work?" Jade asked, still trying to figure that one out.

"As it turns out, Jackson had given your name and number to Trevor. He told him to call you if something ever happens. When Trevor noticed Jackson didn't come back one night, he waited 2 more days, and then he decided to call you." Gavin explained to her.

"I just wish I could have saved Jackson and brought him home to his family." Jade said, with tears forming in her eyes.

"You did, Jade. He's home, he's at rest. You found him, when no one else could. Maybe that was meant to happen." Gavin said, looking Jade in the eyes.

"When I got his belongings, I found a note in his pocket." Jade took it out of her purse and proceeded to read it to Gavin:

Dear Jade,

I'm sure by the time you read this, I'll be gone. I fell in with a wrong crowd. I did some terrible things and I'm not proud of it. I did what I needed to. And don't blame yourself for not coming with me, because I would never have wanted this to happen to you. Tell mom and dad I love them, and I couldn't have asked for better parents. And you, Jade, you are the most wonderful person the world has ever known. Your smile can light up the sky even in the gloomy, Wisconsin, winter weather. I want you to know this is the only way I could get out of what I got myself into. Please don't hold it against me. I may be gone in body, but not in spirit. I'll always be holding your hand.

Love always, Jackson

Jade folded up the letter as neatly as she could and safely tucked it back into her purse. She was not going to let anything happen to it.

"Lathers may not have killed my brother, but he is the reason my brother killed himself. I hope they throw the book at him in Court!" Jade slammed her hands on the table with tears in her eyes.

"I agree, and trust me, he will pay for everything he has done, mark my words!" Gavin said with a stern voice. "This is far from over."

PART 2

Chapter 15

The trial for Michael Lathers, took a lot longer to get started than Jade and her family thought it would. Gavin was either calling or texting her anything he found out, to make sure she and her family were always kept aware of what was going on. They had a tough time with Jury selection, because a lot of people had known Detective Lathers, and not many people had anything bad to say about him.

"How can everybody like him?" Jade asked Gavin the day before the Trial was set to get started.

"Well, he was a Detective. His job was to make people feel safe and that he would always be willing to help. He led two completely different lives, and nobody wants to believe that. Not even his fellow officers on the police department." Gavin told her.

It made Jade sick to her stomach. "What if he actually, somehow, got away with this?" She asked herself. "What if he blamed everything on Cooper?" Jade couldn't help having these questions in her head. She wanted to stay positive, but it was so hard, with the possibility he might walk free.

The night before the trial, Jade and her parents were up half the night, worried about how it was going to go. There was a possibility it could last for weeks, even months, especially with all the testimonies from the other witnesses, besides Jade.

She almost didn't want her parents to go and listen to everything that would be said, especially surrounding Jackson's death. She knew they would show images, and she did not want her parents to go through that. They absolutely refused to stay home, that's where Jade got her stubbornness from, and she couldn't help but smile a little.

"We will be ok sweetheart. We can do this. It's you, I'm worried about." Her dad told her the morning of the start of the trial. "You and Jax, were closer than anybody. Being twins is a special relationship."

"I'll be just fine, Dad. The thought of getting justice for Jackson and all those other people is what's making this a little easier for me." She reassured her father with a smile. Giving one last look in the mirror by the door, she almost thought she saw Jackson looking right back at her, giving her one of his big smiles. They headed outside to wait for their ride to the trial.

Chapter 16

Gavin picked up Jade and her parents on the morning of the trial. When they pulled up to the courthouse Jade was in amazement of how many people were there. She was even more surprised at the signs that some people were holding.

Justice for Jackson.

Justice for Trevor.

Jade had tears in her eyes as she read them. She couldn't believe how many people from their community had come out to support them. But on the negative side, there were a lot of people that were there to support Lathers. Especially from within the police department. Gavin shook his head at the sight.

"We have evidence of what he did, and they all still think he's innocent!" Gavin said rather loudly pulling up to the front steps of the courthouse. "Are they that naïve?"

"Maybe actually seeing the evidence instead of just hearing it, will put things in more perspective for them Gavin." Jade's father said back to him in the front seat. Jade sat and watched her father put a hand on Gavin's shoulder, as a form of comfort.

They stepped out of the suburban and proceeded up the stairs. The attorney for the prosecution met them inside. His name was Daryl Burbank, and he was great. He was good at keeping in contact with Jade and her family as well. He was quite sure they had a win in this case, but you can never know. The defense attorney for Lathers, Jed Medina, was rather good in his own right too.

Both attorneys had an incredibly good reputation within the state of Wisconsin. They had both won and lost their fair share of trials. Jade became familiar with both of them, finding out what she could, when she had heard the names of who the attorneys would be. Gavin reassured her that Mr. Burbank, was the best attorney the prosecution could have gotten.

"I really think Daryl can win this case." Gavin said as we went to sit on the benches in the courtroom. "All the evidence, witnesses, there is just no way we could lose."

"I really hope so, otherwise a lot of families are going to feel let down, if we lose." Jade told him, with her big blue eyes staring at him.

Jade her the words, "All Rise", and they stood up as Judge Deacon Tate, entered the room. He was an older gentleman that Jade had never seen before. She looked him up as well when she found out who would be the judge on

the trial. He had a good reputation as well. She read he could

be a hard ass sometimes, but only to people that deserved it.

She was crossing her fingers that everything would go like she

hoped.

Chapter 17

The trial started with opening statements, where each attorney can give the jury the reasons, the defense is either guilty or not guilty. Opening statements tend to take a long time. They started with Lathers attorney, Mr. Medina:

"Members of the jury, we are here today, to prove that Mr. Michael Lathers is innocent. The defense will do their best to tarnish this Senior Detectives reputation in this community. They will try to encourage you to vote guilty to this "supposed drug producer." But let me ask you: would a detective that has been with the police department for almost 20 years, ruin his reputation that took so long to establish, to produce drugs? Would he be willing to sacrifice his career, his family, his lifestyle, to kidnap some kids off a bus, not knowing they would even be there? Not only that, how can he be to blame for someone's suicide? Continue asking yourself these questions, while the prosecution tries to throw my client under the bus. I hope you will be able to see how this fine, young, detective was not able to accomplish this on his own. He was not the one pulling the strings."

Jade zoned out the rest of Medina's opening statement. When he mentioned Jackson's suicide, Jade's mind went back to finding him in the forest. That's one picture that she can't get out of her mind. Gavin saw the look on her face and grabbed her hand to help support her. Jade in turned grabbed her mother's hand. Medina went back to his seat, when he was finished.

Next up, was the prosecutions, Daryl Burbank's, opening statement:

"Ladies and gentlemen of the jury. Mr. Medina was right, we are here to tarnish this Detectives reputation, because what he has done the last 3 years, is completely, and utterly unbelievable. A Detective, someone that you're supposed to be able to trust, and go to for help, is not only kidnapping kids off a bus, but supplying them with drugs. Then he turns around and has these kids help package them. Does that seem like a Detective that should be looking out for your well-being? The reason he has the lifestyle he does, is because of his little side business he has going on. Do you think he could afford his big house, fancy cars, and expensive vacations, on a police officer's salary? I think not! Not only that, but he also had a young man so tore down, not letting him leave, beating him, drugging him, to the point this young man's only option was suicide. He might not have pulled the trigger, but he was the reason that young man felt he had no other option! I hope once you see all the evidence and witness testimonies, you will make up your own mind, that what Detective Michael Lathers has done, he did on his own. He had no one coercing him or holding a gun to his head. Thank you."

Gavin squeezed Jade's hand and looked at her with a smile, almost like he was telling her that they were going to win. After the opening statements were done, the judge called recess until the next day.

Chapter 18

The next morning came, and Jade was beyond

nervous for her witness testimony. Mr. Burbank had gone

over it with her so many times Jade had lost count. She knew

that Medina would put twice as much pressure on her, since

she's the reason Lathers was found out. They made it to the courthouse by 8am, and the trial started as soon as everyone had arrived. Gavin was called up as the prosecutions first witness.

"Mr. Baxter, can you briefly describe to us, how you became aware of the missing people's cases down in Columbia City?" Burbank asked Gavin.

"We became aware, when we started getting more and more phone calls related to that bus stop. Family members, who were supposed to meet family members there, that never showed up. After doing surveillance and asking neighboring businesses, we were able to zero in on Mr. Cooper Lock. After scoping Mr. Lock out, I was able to put together how he met these young adults at the bar and lured them off the buses." Gavin answered his question.

"How were you able to conclude that Mr. Lathers was involved?" Burbank asked a harder question.

"After hearing that Jackson Winters had went missing 7 months ago, and his sister was very pushy, so to say. She had informed the police department and Mr. Lathers that she planned to go on the same bus route that her brother had taken. I went undercover and followed her, just out of chance, the same instance might occur. I was right, because it did." Gavin fired back, and the attorney told him to step down.

Now was Jade's turn, nervous, walking up to witness box.

"Ms. Winters, can you tell us exactly how you came to be in Columbia City?" Mr. Burbank asked.

"Well, my twin brother went missing 7 months ago now. I wasn't getting anywhere with the police departments between here and New York. I took it upon myself to take the exact same trip, to maybe ask some questions, get some idea where my brother was. I was desperate to find him. The first bus stop was in Columbia City."

Mr. Burbank than asked her questions about the waitress and the bartender she had talked to. She fired back with exactly what happened. Then came the bigger questions.

"What happened after you met Cooper at the bar?" The attorney asked.

"Well, I went to the bathroom, came back, we started dancing, and I started falling asleep out of nowhere. Next thing I know, I'm in his pickup. I tried to get out, he punched me, and then everything went dark. When I came to, we were in the middle of nowhere by a cabin. That's where I saw Detective Michael Lathers. That was where he told me everything about his drug operation. He took me in the basement, to his drug den, and that's where I saw all the young kids packaging his cocaine. I heard the first shots upstairs when the FBI showed up, and I took off running, grabbing who I thought, was my brother, and followed Lathers out of his escape tunnel. When we were outside in the forest, Lathers tried shooting at us, we took off to run, and that's where I tripped over my brother's dead body. Then I realized the young man with me wasn't my brother but someone that looked like him. Then Gavin found us." Jade answered his question, with the best of her memory.

"No further questions your honor." Then Mr. Burbank sat down, while Mr. Medina rose.

"Now Ms. Winters, is it true that your brother has been known to take off before?" Mr. Medina asked Jade with an intimidating look on his face.

"When we were younger, like early 20s, but he would never do that now." Jade fired back.

"Also is it true, that your brother was known to experiment with drugs?" Medina asked. Jade assumed he was trying to get her to get upset, but he didn't know Jade very well.

"No. My brother and I never did any drugs. That was one thing we always promised each other and our parents we would never do." Jade said while looking him straight in the eye.

"Would you say your brother is an easy person to convince, or hardheaded?" The attorney asked Jade.

"No, he's not easy to convince. He's very stubborn and set in his own ways." Jade answered, getting frustrated.

"So, isn't it possible, that it didn't take drugs to get him to cooperate with Cooper? You just said that he's not easy to convince. Isn't it possible he did it on his own, then felt guilty about betraying your trust, and that's why he killed himself?" Medina asked while raising his voice.

"No! My brother would never do such a thing. He would never stoop to those levels. He killed himself because Lathers drugged him, beat him, and he had no other way out!" Jade said raising her voice as well, while staring down Medina, letting him know that she wasn't afraid of him.

"No further questions." Medina walked back to his seat. The judge told Jade to step down and she went back to her seat, next to Gavin.

"You did great Jade." Gavin reassured her.

"I don't feel like I did." Jade said with tears forming in her eyes.

Chapter 19

The other witnesses that were found by Jade and the FBI testified one after another. They all shared the same story.

"I got off the bus in the downtime, and saw a bar, and went and had a drink. I met this fellow named Cooper. Had some drinks, next thing you know, I wake up in this cabin. No idea how I got there, wanting to leave. They beat me a lot, forced drugs down my throat. I felt like a zombie most of the time, and definitely not in my clear mind. When the FBI came, it was like a pot gold at the end of the rainbow. I'm so glad I made it out alive." One witness testified.

Trevor was the last to testify. He had the same story as the rest, but a little more to go with it. Jade listened closely.

"I was there for about a week, I think, before Jackson showed up. The drugs made all the days and times run together. That Jackson, he was a stubborn one, and he was always trying to find a way out, but there was always someone there to stop him. He got beat more than the rest of us and drugged more than us. I remember him telling me if something ever happened to him, to call his sister and he told me her name and gave me her number. One day he tried to get out, and he didn't come back. After 2 days and no

Jackson, I was able to sneak Cooper's cell phone and call his sister. I was only able to leave a voicemail. I'm glad I could do that, because she saved us." He finished while looking at Jade.

Jade had tears in her eyes, and so did her parents. She wanted so badly to run and give Trevor a hug, but she knew it had to wait.

After Trevor's testimony, it was the defenses time for witnesses. They only had a couple that were testifying. They were most members of Lathers family and members of the Green Bay police department, just saying how he was just a good guy, and a great detective, and a dedicated family man. They didn't last too long.

The longest witness testimony was Coopers:

"Mr. Lock, would you say that you are capable of doing what my defendant, Detective Lathers, is charged with?" Medina asking while looking Cooper in the eye.

"Yes, just because I'm not a cop, I think I'd be able to get away with everything he's done." Cooper said back to Mr. Medina.

"In fact, wasn't it you, that orchestrated this whole operation?" Medina asked Cooper while pounding his hands on the witness stand.

"No! Just because I think I'm smart enough to do it, doesn't mean I did it. Lathers has been calling the shots since the very beginning. I told you all that! He found me in that exact same bar and offered me a hell of a percentage if I would be willing to help him get some kids off the bus." Cooper shouted while defending himself.

"You were on drugs yourself weren't you Mr. Lock? How do you know that you weren't hallucinating the whole thing?" Medina counter asked.

"Yes, I do drugs, but not to the point I don't know what the hell I'm doing!" Cooper shouted while standing up.

"No further questions." Medina told the judge while walking back to the table.

"Prosecution rests your Honor." Mr. Burbank said.

"You may step down Mr. Lock." The judge told Cooper.

"Defense rests as well your Honor." Mr. Medina said to the judge while Cooper was walking back to his seat.

When the defense testimonies were done, the judge called recess until the next day. Closing arguments would start tomorrow morning.

Chapter 20

The next morning, closing arguments started. These gave each attorney an opportunity to remind jurors about the key evidence that was presented at the trial. They can also try to persuade to the guilty way or the not guilty way.

Most of the defense's argument was about Lathers years with the police department, and his family, and how the community trusts him. They also tried to shift more of the blame on to Cooper, making the jury believe he was the one that was behind the whole operation. They met Cooper, so they should know he's not that intelligent.

The prosecution had more to share. With the evidence and the witness testimonies, there was just way too much evidence in Jades opinion, for the jury to come back with a not guilty verdict. There was always that chance though. Now it was the jury's time to step out. When they were done, they would call the judge and he would notify the attorneys that they were ready. It could even take days.

When Jade went to sleep that night, she dreamt, but this time it was different. She and Jackson were standing together in the forest.

"Jade, I'm so proud of you. Do you know that?" Jackson asked his sister.

"Jackson, I failed. I didn't get to bring you home. I couldn't save you, when that's all I wanted!" Jade told him, crying.

"But you did bring me home Jade. I'm always with you, mom, and dad. Just remember, wherever you are, I'll be with you." Jackson said while wiping away Jade's tears.

"It's not the same. It'll never be the same." Jade looked at him one last time.

"Jade, all that matters, is I'm home. You did that. You brought all of us home to our families. You saved us. You also stopped it from happening to someone else." Jackson said smiling, and turning around, and vanishing.

Jade slowly opened her eyes. She knew deep in her heart; Jackson was at peace. It would take a while for her to come to terms with the fact that he's gone. Hopefully a guilty verdict for Lathers would help speed up the process.

Chapter 21

It took 2 days, before they got the call that the jury had reached a verdict. It was a long 2 days of Jade and her parents pacing, waiting. When they received the call from the prosecution attorney, Gavin picked Jade and her parents up. The drive felt like it took forever to get to the courthouse. The anticipation of what the jury's verdict would be, was really getting to Jade, her parents, and even to Gavin. She did have to admit that being able to spend so much time with Gavin was worth it. Before they got out of the car, Gavin let Jade's parents out first. He stopped Jade.

"Jade, can I ask you something?" Gavin looked at her.

"Of course, you can Gavin. What's up?" Jade responded.

"I know you've been through a lot. But after this is all over, do you think I could take you out on a proper date, and not just coffee at the café?" Gavin asked.

"I think that would be a great idea. I certainly accept." Jade said while giving him a kiss on the cheek. She grabbed his hand to walk inside the court room.

They sat down after the judge sat down.

"Members of the jury, I appreciate your time spent on looking at all aspects of this case. Have you reached a verdict? The Judge asked.

"We have your honor. We find the defendant, Michael Lathers, guilty of kidnapping, drug distribution, and negligent manslaughter."

There was clapping all around the room. The judge slammed his gavel to quiet people down.

"Thank you, members of the jury, you may step out." The judge instructed. The jury did as they were told and stepped out of the room.

"With the verdict now read, it is my duty to impose punishment. Please stand Mr. Lathers." Lathers did as he was told by the Judge.

"I hereby, sentence you to a term of life in prison. Court adjourned." The judge slammed his gavel again and Lathers put his head in his hands, while the guards came to take him away.

Jade hugged her parents and Gavin. She had tears of happiness flowing from her eyes. Now her brother can really be at peace.

1 Year Later

As Jade walked into her home after a long day of work, it was hard for her to believe that 1 year ago, they were having the trial for her twin brother's killer. Everything changed when she found Jackson. She has finally been able to accept she will never see him alive again, but she still has her dreams and in those she's very much alive. This time, they are the good kind of dreams.

"There's my girl." Gavin came up and kissed her on the lips followed with a great big hug. "I have supper already to go, if you want to take a bubble bath and relax."

"That sounds like a great idea." She winked at him and went to the bathroom. Little did Gavin know that she also had an ulterior motive for wanting to take a bath already so early, she thought while looking at the positive pregnancy test. She was hoping Gavin would be happy, even though they haven't been together very long. They'd only started living together a little over a month ago. They hadn't talked about the subject of babies yet. She finished her bubble bath and came out of the bathroom with a smile on her face.

"Feel better?" Gavin asked looking at her. "You sure have a big smile on your face."

"How much food did you make, because I'm eating for 2 now?" Jade said and she held up the pregnancy test.

Gavin put his hands over his mouth and ran over and picked her up for a great big hug.

"YES!" Gavin screamed while giving Jade a hug and a deep kiss.

After everything called down, and they had a nice supper, they relaxed on the couch thinking of possible baby names.

"If it's a boy I like the name Jackson." Jade said.

"I like that too, and if it's a girl, I like the name Jackie." Gavin told Jade while looking in her deep blue eyes. Jade smiled and kissed him on the lips.

"Jackson, we got it from here." Jade said aloud to herself.

THE END

OTHER WORKS OF J.L.E

Life of a Small Town Girl

About The Author

J.L.E was born and raised in a small town in South Dakota, where she still resides. She's always been an avid reader and just recently got into writing. This is her second book. She self-published her first book, "Life of a Small Town Girl", in July of 2022. When she's not reading or writing, she enjoys photography and spending time with her two dogs, Blaze and Jagger, and her significant other.

Made in the USA
Monee, IL
05 January 2023

24434403R00069